Welcome to ALADDIN QUIX!

If you are looking for fast, fun-to-read stories with colorful characters, lots of kid-friendly humor, easy-to-follow action, entertaining story lines, and lively illustrations, then **ALADDIN QUIX** is for you!

But wait, there's more!

If you're also looking for stories with tables of contents; word lists; about-the-book questions; 64, 80, or 96 pages; short chapters; short paragraphs; and large fonts, then **ALADDIN QUIX** is *definitely* for you!

ALADDIN QUIX: The next step between ready to reads and longer, more challenging chapter books, for readers five to eight years old.

Read all the books in the Royal Sweets series!

ROYAL SWEETS

Save the Unicorns

By Helen Perelman

Illustrated by Olivia Chin Mueller

ALADDIN QUIX

New York   London   Toronto   Sydney   New Delhi

For Stella and Leni, two royal cousins
—H. P.

ALADDIN QUIX
Simon & Schuster Children's Publishing Division
1230 Avenue of the Americas, New York, New York 10020
First Aladdin QUIX hardcover edition May 2022
Text copyright © 2022 by Helen Perelman
Illustrations copyright © 2022 by Olivia Chin Mueller
Also available in an Aladdin QUIX paperback edition.
All rights reserved, including the right of reproduction in whole or in part in any form.
ALADDIN and the related marks and colophon are trademarks of Simon & Schuster, Inc.
For information about special discounts for bulk purchases, please contact
Simon & Schuster Special Sales at 1-866-506-1949
or business@simonandschuster.com.
The Simon & Schuster Speakers Bureau can bring authors to your live event. For more information or to book an event contact the Simon & Schuster Speakers Bureau at 1-866-248-3049 or visit our website at www.simonspeakers.com.
Series designed by Jessica Handelman
Book designed by Tiara Iandiorio
The illustrations for this book were rendered digitally.
The text of this book was set in Archer Medium.
Manufactured in the United States of America 0322 LAK
2 4 6 8 10 9 7 5 3 1
Library of Congress Control Number 2021945985
ISBN 9781534455092 (hc)
ISBN 9781534455085 (pbk)
ISBN 9781534455108 (ebook)

Cast of Characters

Princess Mini: Royal fairy princess of Candy Kingdom

Lady Cherry: Princess Mini's teacher at Royal Fairy Academy

Butterscotch: Princess Mini's royal unicorn

Princess Taffy: Princess Mini's best friend

Chipper: Princess Taffy's royal unicorn

Princess Lolli and Prince Scoop: Princess Mini's parents, ruling royal fairies of Candy Kingdom

Nutley: Royal stable fairy

Lord Licorice: Music teacher at Royal Fairy Academy

Wizard Raylan: Sugar Valley wizard

BonBon: Princess Lolli's unicorn

Gobo: Troll living in Sugar Valley

Prince Frosting and Princess Cupcake: Princess Mini's twin cousins from Cake Kingdom

Lemondrop: A royal unicorn

Sugarpop: Prince Frosting's unicorn

Mocha: Princess Cupcake's unicorn

Contents

1

Red Horn Emergency

"Princess Mini!" Lady Cherry called. "Don't forget your unicorn ribbons!"

It was the end of the school day at Royal Fairy Academy. I stopped at the classroom door

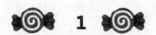

and flew back to my teacher.

"Thank you, Lady Cherry," I said. During the day, my class made colorful licorice ribbons to decorate our unicorns' manes. I couldn't believe I forgot to take my ribbons!

"I am sure **Butterscotch**'s mane will look beautiful tomorrow," Lady Cherry said, smiling. "Have a good time at the Horn Parade!"

"We will!" I said as I flew out the door. "See you at the parade!"

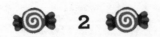 2

Every year the unicorns in Sugar Valley are honored in the Horn Parade. For the first time, my friends and I were going to ride our unicorns in the parade. I was finally old enough!

"Over here, Mini!" Princess Taffy called when I got to the schoolyard. She flew up onto her unicorn, **Chipper**. "I'll race you!"

Princess Taffy is my best friend, and we love racing our unicorns. We were in a hurry to get to my castle. I live in Candy Castle with my parents, **Princess Lolli** and **Prince Scoop**. They are the ruling royal fairies in Candy Kingdom.

"Ready?" I asked. I slipped into Butterscotch's saddle. **"Go!"** I called over my shoulder.

Our unicorns flew over the gates of Royal Fairy Academy and followed Chocolate River to Candy Castle.

"Come on, girl!" I whispered in Butterscotch's ear.

Butterscotch's wide purple

wings flapped hard, and we inched
ahead of Taffy and Chipper.

I could see the candy gardens
and tall candy trees at Candy
Castle. At the top of the castle,

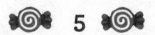

colorful flags waved in the wind.

"Almost there!" I yelled.

Chipper then caught up to Butterscotch. We landed on castle grounds at the same time.

"A tie!" Taffy exclaimed as we landed.

"Good race," I said. I flew off Butterscotch's back.

I opened the **paddock** gate and let Butterscotch and Chipper in. "Come to the stables," I told Taffy. "We can get them a snack."

"School felt so long today,"

Taffy said as she followed me to the barn.

"I know," I said. "All I could think about was the parade tomorrow."

"Me too!" Taffy exclaimed. "Our unicorns are going to look **supersweet**."

"I'm so excited to decorate Butterscotch's mane with the licorice ribbons," I told her. We flew into the barn and took feed bags for our unicorns.

"It took me a long time to get

the colors right," Taffy said. She filled the feed bag with sweet treats. "Chipper will love this candy snack!"

When we returned to the paddock, Butterscotch didn't fly over to me. Usually she knows she is getting a snack and comes right away.

I saw Butterscotch's wings were dragging on the ground.

"Something is wrong," I said to Taffy.

Taffy was stroking Chipper's

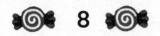

neck. His wings were **drooped** too. "Maybe racing was a bad idea?" she asked.

"Let's get them inside the stable quickly," I told her.

We walked our unicorns over to the barn.

Nutley greeted us. He is the royal stables fairy and takes care of the unicorns.

"Hello, Princess Mini," Nutley said. He took one look at Chipper and Butterscotch and flew into action.

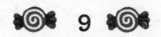

"Bring your unicorns inside," Nutly told us. "Let's give them some water."

"Thank you," I said.

Butterscotch's head was so low, her ears were touching the stable floor.

My wings started to flutter fast. What was wrong with Chipper and Butterscotch?

"Taffy!" I called. **"Look at their horns!"**

Both of our unicorns had red horns!

"What is going on?" I asked. Normally Butterscotch's horn was a pale pink. Now it was as red as a strawberry!

I said, "This is a **red horn emergency**!"

I squeezed Taffy's hand.

She squeezed mine back.

I was red-hot worried!

2

The Wizard

"I am going to send for the wizard," Nutley said. "A red unicorn horn is never a good sign."

"I hope the wizard will know what to do," Taffy said. She hugged Chipper's neck.

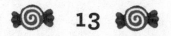

"He will," I replied. I didn't like seeing Butterscotch with a bright red horn. "Poor Butterscotch," I whispered.

"Here," Nutley said, handing us blankets. "Try to keep them warm."

"We should sing a song," I told Taffy. "Sometimes my mom sings to me when I am sick."

"That sounds like a great idea," Taffy said. "**Lord Licorice** taught us that rainbow song in music class yesterday."

We sang out together:

"I can sing a rainbow,

I can sing a rainbow,

red, orange,

yellow, green,

blue, indigo,

and violet!"

The song relaxed Butterscotch and Chipper. They closed their eyes.

"Try to rest," I whispered in Butterscotch's ear.

"Princess Mini!" Nutley called. **"Wizard Raylan** is here."

I turned to see the wizard in his purple robe with silver stars. He had a long white beard and light blue eyes. I met him once at the Candy Ball at the castle. He was a kind wizard who knew all about unicorns.

"Hello, Princess Mini," Raylan said. He tipped his tall purple hat. "Greetings, Princess Taffy."

"Thank you for coming so quickly," I said.

Raylan opened his black bag and took out his silver wand. He

waved the wand over our unicorns. "Hmmm," he said.

"Do you know why their horns
are red?" I asked.

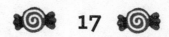

"We raced them home from school today," Taffy said quickly. "I hope that didn't make them sick."

Raylan shook his head. "No," he said. "These unicorns ate something that made them sick." He rubbed his hand up and down his long white beard. "To make them feel better, you must get them rainbow fruit chews."

"Rainbow fruit chews?" I asked. I had only been to Fruit Chew Meadow a couple of times. I didn't remember seeing any rainbow chews.

"We need to **investigate** what the unicorns ate," Raylan said. "But first, let's get them feeling well. Go to Fruit Chew Meadow and get rainbow chews."

"We can get the chews right now," I told Raylan. I looked over at Nutley. "Would you please saddle up **BonBon**?"

"Yes, of course," Nutley said. BonBon was my mother's unicorn, a large lavender unicorn with a dark purple and pink mane.

"The rainbow chews will be in the back corner of the meadow," Raylan told us. He waved his hand, and a scroll appeared. "Here is a map of the meadow," he said. "There are six bushes. Be careful when you pick the rainbow chews because the bushes have **thorns**."

Taffy and I nodded.

"Give two rainbow chews to each unicorn, and send me a sugar fly message when you return," the wizard said.

A sugar fly landed on Raylan's shoulder. He read the note, and his face formed a frown. "Another unicorn has a red horn," he said. He shook his head slowly. "All on the day before the Horn Parade."

"Oh no!" I said.

Raylan put his wand back in his bag. He pet Butterscotch. "Your unicorns should be feeling better as soon as they eat the chews." He tipped his hat. "I hope," he added.

"Thank you, Raylan," I said.

"Give my best to your parents, Princess Mini," he said. He flew out the stables, and in a poof of smoke he was gone.

Nutley appeared with BonBon and her royal saddle.

"We have to hurry," I said to Taffy. We flew up to BonBon's back. "Let's go!"

Leaving Butterscotch was hard, but I had to get the rainbow chews. There was no time to waste!

3

Rainbow Chews

When we got to Fruit Chew Meadow, I took out Raylan's map from my pocket. Taffy and I were standing in front of two tall cherry chew trees, and I found the trees on the map.

"Let's fly this way," I said, pointing to the left. I **traced** my finger along the map. "If we fol-low this path, we will reach the

rainbow chew bushes," I added.

"I didn't know this meadow was so big," Taffy said. "There are so many fruit chew bushes and trees. **I hope we don't get lost!**"

All the bushes and trees were different colors with matching leaves and little chews on the branches. I wanted to try some of the chews, but I knew we had to hurry back to help our unicorns.

I held up the map when we reached an orange bush. "I see the orange bush here," I said. I put my

finger on
the map
and looked
to the right.
"The rainbow chew
bushes should be over
there."

"I see them!" Taffy exclaimed.

I flew up to a branch and carefully pulled off one of the round and striped treats. I saw the sharp thorns Raylan had warned us about.

"Sugar-tastic!" I exclaimed.

"I bet these chews taste as good as they look," Taffy said. She flew next to me with a basket.

"I hope this makes Butterscotch and Chipper feel better," I said. I dropped the chews into the basket.

We picked a basketful of chews and flew back to BonBon.

"Hey, Mini!"

I heard my name being called from a green-and-yellow fruit chew bush. I looked over and saw my troll friend **Gobo** crawling out to say hello.

Gobo lives in Chocolate Woods and is my good friend. I was so surprised to see him in Fruit Chew Meadow.

"Gobo! What are you doing here?" I asked.

4

Red-Hot Mess

"I am meeting **Prince Frosting** and **Princess Cupcake**," Gobo answered.

Just then Frosting landed **Lemondrop** next to the rainbow fruit chew bushes. His twin sis-

ter, Cupcake, was sitting behind him.

"Is everyone searching for rainbow fruit chews?" Frosting asked.

My twin cousins went to Royal Fairy Academy with Taffy and me. We were all in the same class.

"Do your unicorns have red horns too?" Cupcake asked.

"Yes," I said.

"**Sugarpop** and **Mocha** had red horns when we got home from school," Frosting told us. "Raylan came right after seeing you!"

Cupcake looked like she was going to cry.

"Only he didn't give us a map of the meadow," Cupcake whined. Cupcake put her hands on her hips. "He said he gave you one. We thought Gobo might know where the rainbow chews are," she added.

"I do!" Gobo said. He waved his hand in front of the six colorful rainbow chew bushes. "See?"

Cupcake rolled her eyes. "Well, thanks," she said. "I can see that now." She flew over to pick a bunch of chews.

"What do you think made our unicorns sick?" I asked.

Gobo tapped his finger on his chin, thinking. "All your unicorns were in Chocolate Woods yesterday," he said.

"That's right," Frosting said. "We met there after school."

"Maybe they ate something there?" I asked.

"What a red-hot mess," Taffy said, sighing.

"We should go look in Chocolate Woods," Gobo said.

"Good idea, Gobo," I told him. "We will get these rainbow chews to our unicorns and then meet at Chocolate Woods."

"What about tomorrow's parade?" Cupcake asked. "Do you think our unicorns will be better by then?" She dropped a bunch of chews into her basket. "I knew I shouldn't have met you in Chocolate Woods yesterday."

"Cupcake!" Frosting snapped.

"You begged to come for the caramel chocolate treats."

"Well, I didn't think Mocha would get sick," she said, pouting.

"We don't know if anything in Chocolate Woods made them sick," I said.

"I sure hope these chews work fast," Cupcake said. "It would be **super sour** not to fly in our first Horn Parade."

Taffy gave Cupcake a stern look. "We all hope our unicorns

will be better by tomorrow," she said.

"They will be," I said. I held my fingers behind my back tightly crossed, wishing it to be true.

5

Chocolate Woods

At the royal stables, Taffy and I found Butterscotch and Chipper lying on straw beds with blankets over them. Their horns were still bright red.

"Oh, Butterscotch!" I cried.

I flew over to her and gently petted her soft mane. "Here, Raylan says this will help you."

Taffy gave two rainbow chews to Chipper and kissed his neck.

I couldn't take my eyes off Butterscotch's horn.

"I can't help but think we did something to make them sick," Taffy said. She looked up at me with her eyes full of tears.

"I was thinking the same thing," I said.

"Sometimes unicorns get sick," Nutley said, flying into the stable. "Don't worry. These chews should help your unicorns. They will get better. Now, finding what made them sick will help all the unicorns."

I stood up. Nutley was right.

Maybe there were other unicorns who had red horns now too.

"We are going to figure this out," I said. "Nutley, please send a message to Raylan and let him know we gave the unicorns rainbow fruit chews. We will back as soon as we can."

"I will, Princess Mini," Nutley said.

Taffy and I flew BonBon to Chocolate Woods. Cupcake, Gobo, and Frosting were already there. They were searching the area where we ate yesterday.

"We haven't found anything strange," Gobo said.

"Not one clue," Cupcake said.

"Nothing looks **suspicious**," Frosting added.

My friends and I checked all the trees, bushes, and vines in Chocolate Woods. When we were finished, I sat down on a rock and put my head in my hands.

"Maybe the unicorns didn't eat something that made them sick," Cupcake said.

"Raylan was sure the unicorns ate something," I replied. "Let's keep looking."

A tiny sugar fly landed on my shoulder. The note was from

Raylan! I quickly read the message.

"Raylan says he has seen three other sick unicorns," I told my friend.

"Oh no!" Taffy cried.

"Whose unicorns?" Frosting asked.

I continued to read the note. "He says that the other unicorns belong to Prince Bean, Princess Pink, and Princess Gummy," I said. "He still has other unicorns to see too."

"Sour cherries!" Cupcake exclaimed. "The Horn Parade will be canceled if all the unicorns are sick."

"We have to save all the unicorns," I said.

"Wait a minute," Cupcake said. "Those Candy Fairies were not in Chocolate Woods yesterday."

Gobo looked around. "So nothing here would have made your unicorns sick."

"But all those Candy Fairies were at Royal Fairy Academy

yesterday. We all were!" I said.

Frosting snapped his fingers. "The courtyard!" he exclaimed. "We should go there now."

"Gobo," I called. "Come fly with us on BonBon."

"Let's go," Frosting said, flying onto Lemondrop with Cupcake close behind. "We need to get to Royal Fairy Academy fast."

6

Flower Lessons

We left BonBon with Lemondrop outside the front gate of school. **"Don't eat anything!"** I told both unicorns.

I had never been to school after all the students and teachers were gone. I wasn't used to the school-yard being empty—and so quiet!

"What are we looking for?" Taffy asked.

"I guess something a unicorn would eat that looks dangerous," I said.

Gobo walked around the yard. "If you were a unicorn, what would you do here?"

Frosting leaped up in the air and flapped his wings. "I would race around the yard!"

"I would smell the flowers,"

Taffy said, smiling. She pointed to the row of flowers in the back of the yard.

Cupcake twirled her finger around her long blond hair. "I would drink the water from the rainbow fountain," she said. She flew over to the center of the yard where a large fountain sprayed rainbow water from the top.

I stood in the middle of the yard. I tried to think what Butterscotch would do here.

I looked over at the school

building and noticed the Yellow Room window. The Yellow Room was for the first-year students.

"I would try to see inside the classroom," I said. "Sometimes I notice Butterscotch by the window."

Around the window there were tiny red berries and yellow flowers on blue vines, reaching up high and all around the window.

"Hey, everyone," I said. "What do you think this is?"

My friends rushed over.

"Look," Frosting said, pointing.

"The vine is over there, too." He

flew to the next window. "This

is the Blue Room. Prince Bean's class is in the Blue Room."

"I wonder if Raylan knows anything about these vines," I said. "Let's send a sugar fly for him to meet us here."

"Think about how many unicorns are in this yard during the school day," Frosting said. "If they all ate these flowers and berries, this could be a serious problem."

My wings fluttered. "Oh, this is really **bitter bad**," I said.

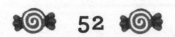

Taffy sighed. "I hope Raylan gets here soon."

"He will," I said. I looked over at the blue vines. How could such pretty flowers and bright berries be so dangerous?

Finally a puff of smoke appeared in the center of the yard.

"I have been all around Sugar Valley," Raylan said. He took off his hat and wiped his forehead. "So many unicorns are sick with red horns."

"Oh, Raylan," I said. "Come

 53

take a look at these vines near the windows." I took Raylan's hand. We flew over to the classroom window.

Raylan looked closely at the vines. He stroked his long beard and shook his head. **"Oh no!** These are **poisonous** flowers!" he cried.

7

Sugar Flies

"This is worse than I thought," Raylan said. "How many unicorns were in the schoolyard today?"

"I'm not sure," I told him. "Everyone flies to school on their unicorns."

"We need to reach all the students at Royal Fairy Academy," Raylan said. "They must check on their unicorns immediately!"

My heart sank. Candy Fairies came from all over Sugar Valley to attend Royal Fairy Academy. Some Candy Fairies traveled very far each day.

"We have to tell everyone, and fast!" Frosting exclaimed.

"There are so many Candy Fairies and unicorns!" Cupcake said. "We have to save *all* the unicorns! How will we do that?"

Just as Cupcake spoke, a sugar fly landed on my shoulder.

"It's a note from Nutley!" I cried. My wings started moving fast.

"Read the note!" Taffy said. "Is everything all right?"

My hands were shaking as I read: "Butterscotch and Chipper are doing well. Their horns are not red anymore."

"Does that mean what I think it means?" asked Frosting.

"Yes," I answered. **"The rainbow chews worked!"**

My friends cheered.

I saw Raylan smile.

And then, I had a **sugar-tastic** idea!

"We should write sugar fly notes to all the Royal Fairy Academy students," I said.

"Good thinking," Raylan said.

Suddenly a beautiful golden unicorn landed in the schoolyard.

It was Lady Cherry! Our Yellow Room teacher!

"Hello, students," Lady Cherry called. "I heard about what happened. I came to help." She flew off her unicorn and held a thick scroll. "Here are the names of all the students at Royal Fairy Academy."

My friends and I started writing sugar fly notes as fast as we could. We told the students to see if their unicorns had red horns and to go to Fruit Chew Meadow for help. There were many names on Lady Cherry's scroll, but we

sent a note to every student.

"Let's go back to Fruit Chew Meadow," Cupcake said. "We can have the rainbow chews ready for

Candy Fairies who needs some."

"That is a **rainbow-licious** idea!" I exclaimed.

I smiled at Cupcake. Sometimes she could be very sweet.

The sugar flies lined up and took the notes to Royal Fairy Academy students all over Sugar Valley.

There wasn't a moment to lose!

8

Perfect Pink

As soon as we finished up the sugar fly notes, my friends and I flew back to Fruit Chew Meadow. We picked baskets full of rainbow chews and waited for Candy Fairies to come.

The students made a line, and we handed out chews for their unicorns. We made a great team.

"I think we saw *every* student at Royal Fairy Academy," I said. I sat down on the ground near a cherry fruit chew tree.

"The sugar flies got the message out fast," Gobo said. He sat down next to me.

"We picked every rainbow fruit chew on those bushes," Taffy added.

"And I have the scratches to prove it!" Cupcake exclaimed,

holding up her hands. She smiled. "But I am glad that I could help."

Raylan appeared in a puff of smoke. "Excellent job, Candy Fairies," he said. **"You have saved the unicorns!"**

"No more red horns?" I asked.

"Not in Sugar Valley," Raylan said happily. "And those vines were taken down from the school courtyard."

My friends and I gave a cheer.

"Now all the unicorns will be able to ride in the Horn Parade," I said.

Cupcake grinned. "Our very first parade!" She looked over at Frosting. "Come on, we have to get ready!" She took Frosting's hand and dragged him to Lemondrop.

Frosting rolled his eyes. "The parade is tomorrow," he said. "You have plenty of time!"

"Do I?" Cupcake asked. "There is so much to do!"

"We'll see you tomorrow at the parade," Frosting called.

"Yes!" I said.

"Let's go see Butterscotch

and Chipper," Taffy said.

BonBon flew Taffy and me back to Candy Castle. Butterscotch and Chipper looked great! Their horns were pink and they were flying around the paddock.

"Hello, Princess Lolli," Taffy said when she saw my mother.

"You have done a great job today," my mom said. "Lady Cherry came to see me and told me what was happening. She told me what a wonderful job you and your friends did for all the unicorns."

"I am so happy that the unicorns are better," I said, petting Butterscotch's neck. "Butterscotch's horn is back to being perfect pink!"

68

"The Horn Parade will happen tomorrow, right?" Taffy asked my mom.

"Yes, sure as sugar!" my mom replied. "Tomorrow morning there will be an extra-special Horn Parade!"

9

Rainbow Ready

The next morning I met Taffy at the royal stables. Taffy had her licorice ribbons with her.

"I love your dress," I told Taffy, giggling. We were wearing the same dress! We had planned our

matching outfits for months. Our dresses had sparkling rows of rainbow colors and tiny rainbow sprinkles across the neckband.

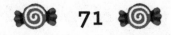

"I can't believe this day is finally here," Taffy said. She took one long licorice ribbon and braided part of Chipper's mane.

"I know!" I said. I reached for a pink licorice ribbon and started to braid Butterscotch's long pink mane. "Oh, Butterscotch," I said when I finished. "You look better than a rainbow fruit chew!"

Taffy laughed. "They both look **sugar-tastic**!"

Just then, Frosting and Cupcake

flew into the paddock on their uni-corns.

"Hello!" Frosting called.

Gobo was seated on Sugarpop's back next to Frosting. He waved.

"Frosting said I could ride with him," he said, grinning. "Do you think that is okay?"

"Sure as sugar!" I cried.

"I love your hat," Taffy said to Gobo. He was wearing a rainbow top hat. He looked very proud.

"You all look amazing and **rainbow-licious**!" I said, smiling.

Cupcake was wearing a rainbow dress with a rainbow cotton candy puff at the bottom. Frosting was wearing a rainbow jacket and tie.

"Are you ready?" Cupcake asked.

"I can't wait for the parade to start!" Taffy said.

"Me too," I said. "We all look rainbow ready!"

We flew our unicorns to the front lawn at the castle. There were rainbow flags lining the castle gardens. My mother was standing on a platform surrounded by castle guards with long, shiny horns. There were many Candy Fairies waiting for the parade to begin.

"I am a little nervous. Are you?" Taffy asked. She looked around at all the Candy Fairies.

"We will stay together," I said. I felt brave on Butterscotch's back.

"Welcome to the Horn Parade!" my mother said to the crowd.

There was a loud cheer from all

 75

the Candy Fairies. I looked over at my friends and their unicorns. Not one unicorn had a red horn!

"Before we start the parade," my mother said, "I would like to present a special award to the four first-years at Royal Fairy Academy and their friend Gobo.

"Without their help," she continued, "we would not have found the reason for our red-horned unicorns. They sent out sugar fly notes to let everyone know to get rainbow chews to help the unicorns.

They saved all the unicorns!"

My mother also thanked Raylan and called him up to the stage. "To our wonderful wizard," she said. "He knew exactly what our unicorns needed!"

Raylan held a long staff. He was **beaming** with pride as he lowered the staff to signal the start of the parade. The castle guards blew their horns.

"Let the parade begin!" Raylan called out. "Give a cheer for our unicorns!"

My friends and I waved to the crowd. I leaned down and hugged Butterscotch's neck. Her mane looked perfect in braids with colorful licorice ribbons.

"I am so happy you are okay," I whispered in her ear.

Butterscotch shook her head and flew next to Chipper.

"This is a **supersweet** day

for all unicorns!" I said. "This is the best Horn Parade ever!" I looked over at my friends. We were flying through all the kingdoms in Sugar Valley on our unicorns. It was a big celebration!

"I am lucky to have the best friends," I said. I kissed Butterscotch's neck. "And I have the sweetest unicorn with a perfect pink horn!"

Word List

beaming (BEEM·ing): Smiling widely, happily

drooped (DROOPT): Hung down low

investigate (in·VESS·tuh·gate): To look into carefully

paddock (PA·duck): An area surrounded by a fence where animals exercise

poisonous (POY·zun·us): Likely to cause harm

suspicious (suh·SPI·shus): Raising questions

thorns (THORNZ): Sharp points on a flower or bush stem

traced (TRAYST): Followed along the line

Questions

1. What made the unicorns sick?
2. Have you ever had to take care of a sick animal?
3. What would you wear to the Horn Parade?
4. If you had a unicorn, what colors would the unicorn's mane, tail, and body be? What would the unicorn's name be?

LOOKING FOR A FAST, FUN READ?
BE SURE TO MAKE IT ALADDIN QUIX!